The story of David and Goliath is retold
in this delightfully simple version and will
appeal to all young listeners and early readers.
The story is based on the First Book of Samuel,
chapters 16 and 17.

British Library Cataloguing in Publication Data
Murdock, Hy
    David. — (Ladybird Bible stories)
    1. David, *King of Israel* — Juvenile literature
    2. Bible stories. English — O.T.
    I. Title   II. Grundy, Lynn N.
    221.9'.24   BS580.D3
    ISBN 0-7214-9520-6

First Edition

Published by Ladybird Books Ltd Loughborough Leicestershire UK
Ladybird Books Inc Lewiston Maine 04240 USA
© LADYBIRD BOOKS LTD MCMLXXXV
© Illustrations LYNN N GRUNDY MCMLXXXV

David

written by HY MURDOCK
illustrated by LYNN N GRUNDY

Ladybird Books

Saul was King of Israel. But he hadn't always been a good King and he had made God angry. Saul knew this and he became more unhappy and more bad tempered. Sometimes he was so angry that his servants were afraid. One of them asked Saul if he would like to hear gentle music to make him feel better. King Saul agreed.

The servant remembered that David the shepherd boy played the harp very beautifully so David came to Saul's palace and played for the King whenever he felt angry and upset.

For many years the people of Israel had been fighting against the Philistines who lived nearby. Now there was going to be another big battle.

King Saul and the Israelite army were on a mountain on one side of a valley called Elah. The huge Philistine army was ready on the mountain on the other side of the valley. They waited and waited for the battle to begin.

One day a great tall Philistine called
Goliath came down the hillside to speak
to the Israelite army. He said that if one
Israelite could fight him and beat him
then there need not be a battle. If he
was beaten the Philistines would
become servants of Israel.

The Israelites were afraid. Goliath was like a giant and was covered in armour. He had a shield, a big sword and an enormous spear.

David had gone back home to see his father and to look after the sheep but three of his older brothers had gone to fight in Saul's army. One day David's father asked him to go and see his brothers and to take food to them.

When David got there he saw the giant Goliath and his brothers told him what was happening. Goliath had shouted across the valley every morning and every evening for forty days but no Israelite was brave enough to fight him.

David went to King Saul and said that
he would go and fight Goliath. But Saul
said David was too young and that he
couldn't fight a man as big as Goliath.
David told Saul that when he was
looking after the sheep he had fought
lions and bears and God had looked
after him.

Saul knew that God would help David and so he gave him some armour to wear. David said that he couldn't wear the heavy armour. Instead he took his staff and his sling. He chose five smooth stones from the river and put them in his pouch.

David walked across the valley. When Goliath saw him coming he laughed and shouted about the Israelites sending a boy to fight for them. David replied that he wasn't afraid because he had God to help him. Then Goliath came down the mountain towards David.

As Goliath came nearer, David took one stone and put it in his sling. Then he took aim and sent the stone flying towards Goliath.

It hit Goliath on his forehead and the giant fell to the ground. David picked up Goliath's sword and chopped off the Philistine's head.

When the Philistine army saw this they
ran away. David had saved the
Israelites from a terrible battle.